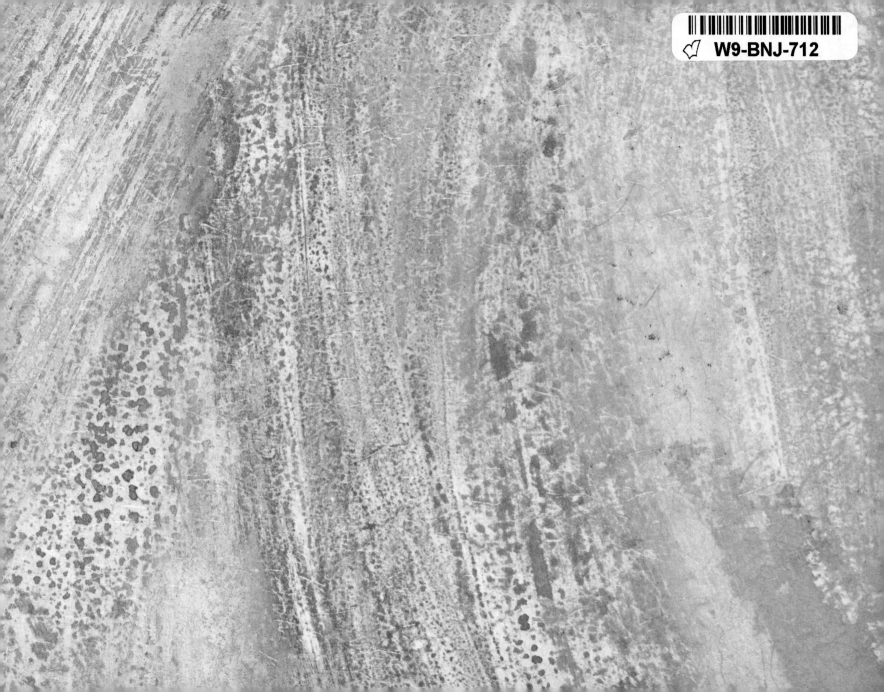

THE MAGIC CAROUSEL

The Magic Carousel

By Dorothy Levenson · Illustrated by Ati Forberg

PARENTS' MAGAZINE PRESS · NEW YORK

Other Books by Dorothy Levenson

The Day Joe Went to the Supermarket
Too Many Pockets
One Kitten Is Not Too Many

*

*To Dana and Lisa who live in New York City
and loved to ride the carousel when they
were little girls.*

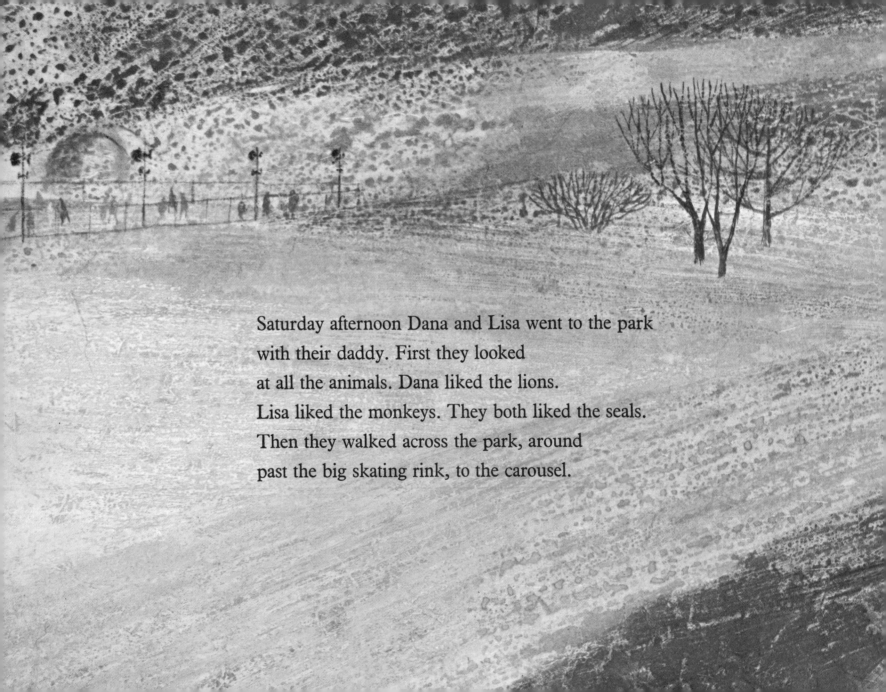

Saturday afternoon Dana and Lisa went to the park
with their daddy. First they looked
at all the animals. Dana liked the lions.
Lisa liked the monkeys. They both liked the seals.
Then they walked across the park, around
past the big skating rink, to the carousel.

Daddy bought the tickets. He gave them
to Dana to hold because she was almost five.
Lisa was only three and might drop them.
They watched the carousel go round. The horses
whirled and dipped and lifted their heads.
Round and round and round. Up and down
and round and round.

When the carousel stopped, Lisa and Dana
got on. Daddy lifted Lisa up. Dana
climbed on herself
and Daddy fixed the straps.
Dana gave the tickets
to the ticket collector when he came.
Daddy stepped down
and the carousel started.

Lisa held very tight with both hands
and looked straight ahead
because she was small.
But Dana sat up very straight
and waved to Daddy
each time they went past.
In the beginning the horses
went slowly—dipping and lifting
their heads—going round and round.

The music played, faster and faster.

Round and round went the horses, faster and faster.

The wind blew through Dana's hair,

faster and faster.

The wind blew Lisa's long blue hair ribbon

out behind her.

Faster and faster.

Round and round.

Up and down.

The two big black horses lifted their black heads
higher and higher. They flashed their golden eyes.
They sniffed with their golden noses.
Round and round went the big black horses,
lifting their heads higher and higher,
flashing their golden eyes,
sniffing with their golden noses.

Then—*woosh!* Down went their heads and up went
their heels and away they jumped. Off the carousel,
away from the carousel, over the grass
and through the park. Lisa held on very tight
with both hands and looked straight ahead
because she was small. But Dana sat up very straight
and looked at everything they went past.

The horses galloped fast—kicking up
their heels and *clip-clopping*
on the pathways. They *clip-clopped*
through the tunnel and up the hill
where the old men played chess.

They pranced and danced over the grass
to the skating rink. They galloped
around the skating rink three times
while all the skaters waved and shouted.
All except a little girl who had
a short red dress and was skating slowly
on one leg, with the other leg
held out behind.
Dana's horse was in front and she had
to look behind to see Lisa's blue hair ribbon
blowing out along the wind.

Faster and faster went the horses.
Up and down went their heads. Past the zoo
they galloped. The lions roared
when they saw them. The monkeys chattered.
The seals barked. The people in the
restaurant rushed to the windows
with their hot dogs in their hands.
They wanted to see, too.

Up the steps clattered the horses. On they swept
onto the Avenue. Everyone was surprised
to see two little girls in blue coats
riding two big black horses with golden eyes.
Cars tooted and taxis honked. Two big green buses
pulled over to the curb and let them pass.
All the men with gold braid on their coats
who opened apartment house doors
saluted as they went past. Dana saw them all.

Down the Avenue they galloped,
past the biggest toy store in the world.
The dolls and animals in the window waved
to the horses. Dana waved back
but Lisa held on tight.

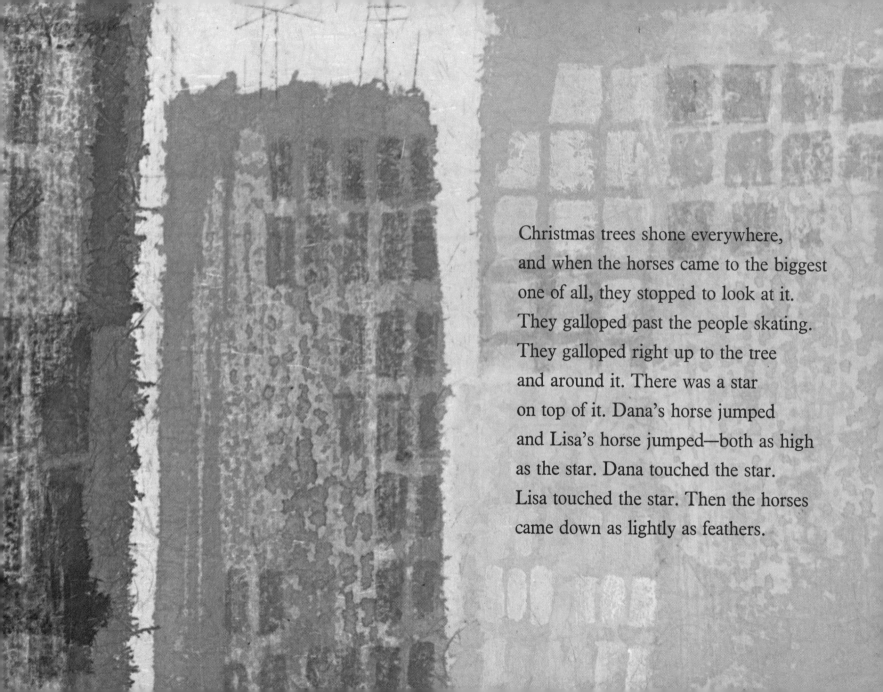

Christmas trees shone everywhere,
and when the horses came to the biggest
one of all, they stopped to look at it.
They galloped past the people skating.
They galloped right up to the tree
and around it. There was a star
on top of it. Dana's horse jumped
and Lisa's horse jumped—both as high
as the star. Dana touched the star.
Lisa touched the star. Then the horses
came down as lightly as feathers.

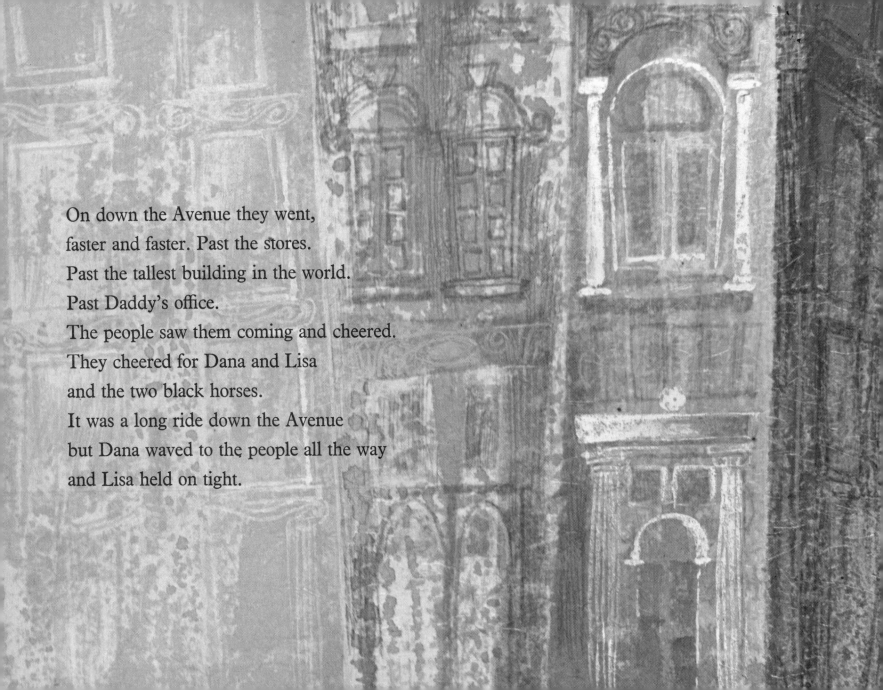

On down the Avenue they went,
faster and faster. Past the stores.
Past the tallest building in the world.
Past Daddy's office.
The people saw them coming and cheered.
They cheered for Dana and Lisa
and the two black horses.
It was a long ride down the Avenue
but Dana waved to the people all the way
and Lisa held on tight.

At last they came to Washington Square.
Dana and Lisa often played there
because they lived nearby, in a house
with lots of stairs. They had watched
the workmen putting up the Christmas tree
in Washington Square,
and they wanted to show it to the horses.
They pulled on the reins and the horses
galloped under the arch—*clip, clop.*
They stopped and stared at the tree
because it was the prettiest of any
they had seen.

But now it was time to go back
to the carousel. Dana and Lisa
pulled on the reins again.
The horses wheeled. They galloped
out of Washington Square.
Up the Avenue they went—
past Daddy's office,
past the tallest building in the world,
past the glittering stores,
past the Christmas trees.
Dana and Lisa looked at the biggest
tree of all as they went past
and thought how they had touched the star.
All the dolls and animals waved again
and then they were back at the park.

The horses were tired now after their long gallop.
They went slower and slower, and their golden eyes
were losing their shine. Once more the lions
roared, the monkeys chattered, the seals barked
and the people waved to the horses as they
went through the zoo. Past the skating rink
they went, where the little girl in the red dress
was still skating on one leg. Up and over the hill,
whoosh! They jumped back on the carousel.

The carousel went slower and slower.
The music went slower and slower.
The music stopped and the carousel stopped.
Daddy came up to help with the straps.
He lifted Lisa down.
Then they all went home, down the Avenue
in a green bus. Dana and Lisa told Daddy
about their long ride, but Dana told
the most because Lisa was only three.

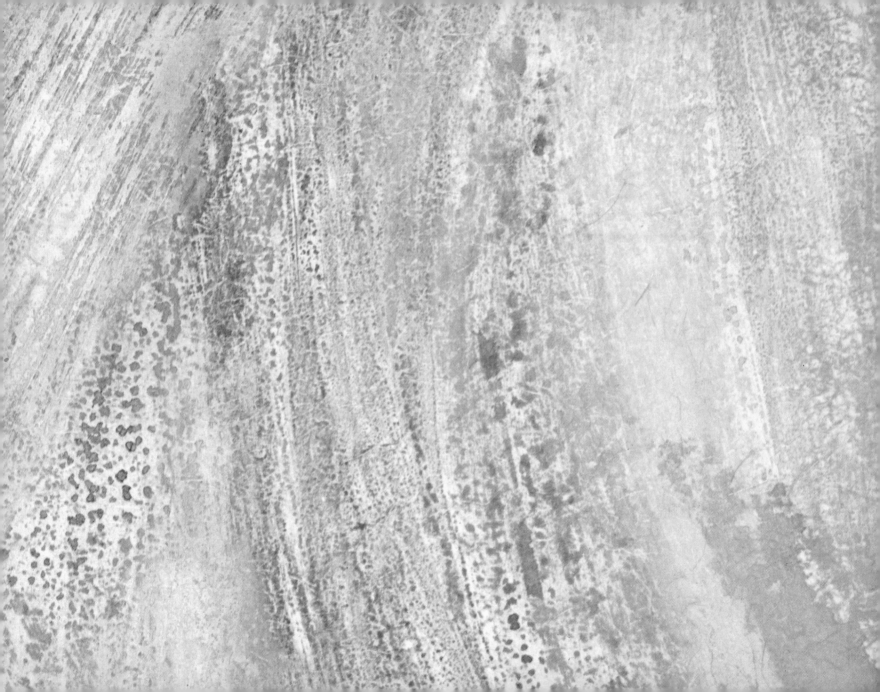